This Is the Sunflower

By **Lola M. Schaefer**

Pictures by Donald Crews

Greenwillow Books
An Imprint of HarperCollinsPublishers

This is the sunflower,
tall and bright,

that stands in my garden
day and night.

This is the blossom,
yellow and round,
that crowns the sunflower,
tall and bright,

that stands in my garden
day and night.

These are the seeds,
black and brown,
found in the blossom,
yellow and round,
that crowns the sunflower,
tall and bright,
that stands in my garden
day and night.

These are the beaks,
sharp and strong,
that crack the seeds,
black and brown,
found in the blossom,

yellow and round,
that crowns the sunflower,
tall and bright,
that stands in my garden
day and night.

**These are the birds,
full of song,
that use their beaks,
sharp and strong,**

to crack the seeds,
black and brown,
found in the blossom,
yellow and round,
that crowns the sunflower,
tall and bright,
that stands in my garden
day and night.

Here are a few seeds
scattered around,
spilled by the birds,
full of song,
that use their beaks,
sharp and strong,
to crack the seeds,
black and brown,
found in the blossom,
yellow and round,
that crowns the sunflower,
tall and bright,
that stands in my garden
day and night.

Now the sun warms
the moist ground
that covers the seeds
scattered around,
spilled by the birds,
full of song,
that use their beaks,
sharp and strong,
to crack the seeds,
black and brown,
found in the blossom,
yellow and round,
that crowns the sunflower,
tall and bright,
that stands in my garden
day and night.

**These are the sprouts,
rich with life, that grow**

and grow
and **grow** until...

a patch of sunflowers,
tall and bright,

**stands in my garden
day and night.**

These are the the birds, full of song, found in this book

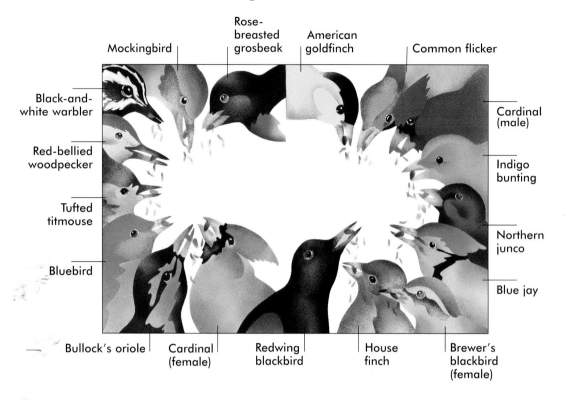

Mockingbird · Rose-breasted grosbeak · American goldfinch · Common flicker · Black-and-white warbler · Red-bellied woodpecker · Tufted titmouse · Bluebird · Cardinal (male) · Indigo bunting · Northern junco · Blue jay · Bullock's oriole · Cardinal (female) · Redwing blackbird · House finch · Brewer's blackbird (female)

SUNFLOWER FACTS: Sunflowers are large, bright flowers of yellow, orange, or dark red. They bloom in late summer and autumn and can grow to be three feet across and more than fifteen feet tall. Hundreds of seeds grow in the center of each sunflower.
Every part of the sunflower can be used. The petals can be used as a dye; the seeds can be used as food for birds, poultry, and people, or for making cooking oils and oils for soaps and candles; and even the stems can be used for making papers and textiles.

For Nick, who helps me see the wonder in life—L. M. S.

For Jack—May 1, 1999, something to grow on—D. C.

Watercolors were used for the full-color art.
The text type is Futura Bold.

Printed in Singapore by Tien Wah Press.
All rights reserved.
http://harperchildrens.com

Library of Congress Cataloging-in-Publication Data

Schaefer, Lola M., (date)
This is the sunflower / by Lola M. Schaefer ; illustrations by Donald Crews.
   p.   cm.
"Greenwillow Books."
Summary: A cumulative verse describing how a sunflower in a garden blossoms and, with the help of the birds, spreads its seeds to create an entire patch of sunflowers.
ISBN 0-688-16413-7 (trade)
ISBN 0-688-16414-5 (lib. bdg.)
[1. Sunflowers—Fiction.
2. Birds—Fiction.]
I. Crews, Donald, ill.
II. Title. PZ7.S33233Th
2000   [E]—dc21
98-46682   CIP   AC

10 9 8 7 6 5 4 3 2 1
First Edition